PISTOL POLITICS

BY

ROBERT E. HOWARD

British Library Cataloguing-in-Publication Data
A catalogue record for this book is available from the
British Library

Robert E. Howard

Robert Ervin Howard was born in Peaster, Texas in 1906. During his youth, his family moved between a variety of Texan boomtowns, and Howard – a bookish and somewhat introverted child – was steeped in the violent myths and legends of the Old South. Although he loved reading and learning, Howard developed a distinctly Texan, hardboiled outlook on the world. He became a passionate fan of boxing, taking it up at an amateur level, and from the age of nine began to write adventure tales of semi-historical bloodshed. In 1919, when Howard was thirteen, his family moved to the Central Texas hamlet of Cross Plains, where he would stay for the rest of his life.

At fifteen Howard began to read the pulp magazines of the day, and to write more seriously. The December 1922 issue of his high school newspaper featured two of his stories, 'Golden Hope Christmas' and 'West is West'. In 1924 he sold his first piece – a short caveman tale titled 'Spear and Fang' – for $16 to the not-yet-famous *Weird Tales* magazine. He published with the magazine regularly over the next few years. 1929 was a breakout year for Howard, in that the 23-year-old writer began to sell to other magazines, such as *Ghost Stories* and *Argosy,* both of whom had previously sent him hundreds of rejection slips. In 1930, he began a correspondence with weird fiction master H. P. Lovecraft which ran up to his death six years later, and is regarded as one of the great correspondence cycles in all of fantasy literature.

It was partly due to Lovecraft's encouragement that Howard created his most famous character, Conan the Cimmerian. Conan – a barbarian-turned-King during the Hyborian Age, a mythical period of some 12,000 years ago – featured in seventeen *Weird Tales* stories between 1933 and 1936, and is now regarded as having spawned the 'sword and sorcery' genre, making Howard's influence on fantasy literature comparable to that of J. R. R. Tolkien's. The Conan stories have since been adapted many times, most famously in the series of films starring Arnold Schwarzenegger.

Howard was enjoying an all-time high in sales by the beginning of 1936, but he was also deeply upset by the ill health of his mother, who had fallen into a coma. On the morning of June 11, 1936, he asked an attending nurse whether she would ever recover, and the nurse replied negatively. Howard walked to his car, parked outside the family home in Cross Plains, and shot himself. He died eight hours later, aged just thirty.

Politics and book-learning is bad enough took separate; together they're a blight and a curse. Take Yeller Dog for a instance, a mining camp over in the Apache River country, where I was rash enough to take up my abode in onst.

Yeller Dog was a decent camp till politics reared its head in our midst and education come slithering after. The whiskey was good and middling cheap. The poker and faro games was honest if you watched the dealers clost. Three or four piddlin' fights a night was the usual run, and a man hadn't been shot dead in more than a week by my reckoning. Then, like my Aunt Tascosa Polk would say, come the deluge.

It all begun when Forty-Rod Harrigan moved his gambling outfit over to Alderville and left our one frame building vacant, and Gooseneck Wilkerson got the idee of turning it into a city hall. Then he said we ought to have a mayor to go with it, and announced hisself as candidate. Naturally Bull Hawkins, our other leading citizen, come out agen him. The election was sot for April 11. Gooseneck established his campaign headquarters in the Silver Saddle saloon, and Bull taken up his'n in the Red Tomahawk on t'other side of the street. First thing we knowed, Yeller Dog was in the grip of politics.

The campaign got under way, and the casualties was mounting daily as public interest become more and more

3

fatally aroused, and on the afternoon of the 9th Gooseneck come into his headquarters. and says: "We got to make a sweepin' offensive, boys. Bull Hawkins is outgeneralin' us. That shootin' match he put on for a prime beef steer yesterday made a big hit with the common herd. He's tryin' to convince Yeller Dog that if elected he'd pervide the camp with more high-class amusement than I could. Breck Elkins, will you pause in yore guzzlin' and lissen here a minute? As chief of this here political organization I demand yore attention!"

"I hear you," I says. "I was to the match, and they barred me on a tecknicality, otherwise I would of won the whole steer. It warn't so excitin', far as I could see. Only one man got shot."

"And he was one of my voters," scowled Gooseneck. "But we got to outshine Bull's efforts to seduce the mob. He's resortin' to low, onder-handed tactics by buyin' votes outright. I scorns sech measures--anyway, I've bought all I'm able to pay for. We got to put on a show which out-dazzles his dern' shootin' match."

"A rodeo, maybe," suggested Mule McGrath. "Or a good dog-fight."

"Naw, naw," says Gooseneck. "My show will be a symbol of progress and culture. We stages a spellin' match tomorrow night in the city hall. Next mornin' when the polls opens the voters'll still be so dazzled by the grandeur of our entertainment they'll eleck me by a vast majority."

"How many men in this here camp can spell good enough to git into a spellin' bee?" says I.

"I'm confident they's at least thirty-five men in this camp which can read and write," says Gooseneck. "That's plenty. But we got to find somebody to give out the words. It wouldn't look right for me--it'd be beneath my offishul dignity. Who's educated enough for the job?"

"I am!" says Jerry Brennon and Bill Garrison simultaneous. They then showed their teeth at each other. They warn't friends nohow.

"Cain't but one git the job," asserted Gooseneck. "I tests yore ability. Can either one of you spell Constantinople?"

"K-o-n--" begun Garrison, and Brennon burst into a loud and mocking guffaw, and said something pointed about ignoramuses.

"You $%#&*!" says Garrison blood-thirstily.

"Gentlemen!" squawked Gooseneck--and then ducked as they both went for their guns.

* * *

THEY CLEARED LEATHER about the same time. When the smoke oozed away Gooseneck crawled out from under the roulette table and cussed fervently.

"Two more reliable voters gone to glory!" he raged. "Breckinridge, whyn't you stop 'em?"

"'T'warn't none of my business," says I, reaching for another drink, because a stray bullet had knocked my glass out a my hand. "Hey!" I addressed the barkeep sternly. "I see you fixin' to chalk up that there spilt drink agen me. Charge it to Jerry Brennon. He spilt it."

"Dead men pays no bills," complained the bartender.

"Cease them petty squabbles!" snarled Gooseneck. "You argys over a glass of licker when I've jest lost two good votes! Drag 'em out, boys," he ordered the other members of the organization which was emerging from behind the bar and the whiskey barrels where they'd took refuge when the shooting started. "Damn!" says Gooseneck with bitterness. "This here is a deadly lick to my campaign! I not only loses two more votes, but them was the best educated men in camp, outside of me. Now who we goin' to git to conduck the spellin' match?"

"Anybody which can read can do it," says Lobo Harrison a hoss-thief with a mean face and a ingrown disposition. He'd go a mile out of his way jest to kick a dog. "Even Elkins there could do it."

"Yeah, if they was anything to read from," snorted Gooseneck. "But they ain't a line of writin' in camp except on whiskey bottles. We got to have a man with a lot of long words in his head. Breckinridge, dammit, jest because I told the barkeep to charge yore drinks onto campaign expenses

6

ain't no reason for you to freeze onto that bar permanent. Ride over to Alderville and git us a educated man."

"How'll he know whether he's educated or not?" sneered Lobo, which seemed to dislike me passionately for some reason or another.

"Make him spell Constantinople," says Gooseneck.

"He cain't go over there," says Soapy Jackson. "The folks has threatened to lynch him for cripplin' their sheriff."

"I didn't cripple their fool sheriff," I says indignantly. "He crippled hisself fallin' through a wagon wheel when I give him a kind of a push with a rock. How you spell that there Constance Hopple word?"

Well, he spelt it thirty or forty times till I had it memorized, so I rode over to Alderville. When I rode into town the folks looked at me coldly and bunched up and whispered amongst theirselves, but I paid no attention to 'em. I never seen the deputy sheriff, unless that was him I seen climbing a white oak tree as I hove in sight. I went into the White Eagle saloon and drunk me a dram, and says to the barkeep: "Who's the best educated man in Alderville?"

Says he: "Snake River Murgatroyd, which deals monte over to the Elite Amusement Palace." So I went over there and jest as I went through the door I happened to remember that Snake River had swore he was going to shoot me on sight next time he seen me, account of some trouble we'd had over a card game. But sech things is too trivial to bother about. I went up to where he was setting dealing monte, and I says: "Hey!"

"Place your bet," says he. Then he looked up and said: "You! $#/0&*@!" and reched for his gun, but I got mine out first and shoved the muzzle under his nose.

"Spell Constantinople!" I tells him.

He turnt pale and said: "Are you crazy?"

"Spell it!" I roared, and he says: "C-o-n-s-t-a-n-t-i-n-o-p-l-e! What the hell?"

"Good," I said, throwing his gun over in the corner out of temptation's way. "We wants you to come over to Yeller Dog and give out words at a spellin' match."

EVERYBODY IN THE PLACE was holding their breath. Snake River moved his hands nervous-like and knocked a jack of diamonds off onto the floor. He stooped like he was going to pick it up, but instead he jerked a bowie out of his boot and tried to stab me in the belly. Well, much as I would of enjoyed shooting him, I knowed it would spile the spelling match, so merely taken the knife away from him, and held him upside down to shake out whatever other weppins he might have hid, and he begun to holler: "Help! Murder! Elkins is killin' me!"

"It's a Yeller Dog plot!" somebody howled, and the next instant the air was full of beer mugs and cuspidors. Some of them spittoons was quite heavy, and when one missed me

and went bong on Snake River's head, he curled up like a angleworm which has been tromped on.

"Lookit there!" they hollered, like it was my fault. "He's tryin' to kill Snake River! Git him, boys!"

They then fell on me with billiard sticks and chair laigs in a way which has made me suspicious of Alderville's hospitality ever since.

Argyment being useless, I tucked Snake River under my left arm and started knocking them fool critters right and left with my right fist, and I reckon that was how the bar got wrecked. I never seen a bar a man's head would go through easier'n that'n. So purty soon the survivors abandoned the fray and run out of the door hollering: "Help! Murder! Rise up, citizens! Yeller Dog is at our throats! Rise and defend yore homes and loved ones!"

You would of thought the Apaches was burning the town, the way folks was hollering and running for their guns and shooting at me, as I clumb aboard Cap'n Kidd and headed for Yeller Dog. I left the main road and headed through the bresh for a old trail I knowed about, because I seen a whole army of men getting on their hosses to lick out after me, and while I knowed they couldn't catch Cap'n Kidd, I was a feared they might hit Snake River with a stray bullet if they got within range. The bresh was purty thick and I reckon it was the branches slapping him in the face which brung him to, because all to onst he begun hollering blue murder.

"You ain't takin' me to Yeller Dog!" he yelled. "You're takin' me out in the hills to murder me! Help! Help!"

"Aw, shet up," I snorted. "This here's a short cut."

"You can't get across Apache River unless you follow the road to the bridge," says he.

"I can, too," I says. "We'll go acrost on the foot-bridge."

With that he give a scream of horror and a convulsive wrench which tore hisself clean out of his shirt which I was holding onto. The next thing I knowed all I had in my hand was a empty shirt and he was on the ground and scuttling through the bushes. I taken in after him, but he was purty tricky dodging around stumps and trees, and I begun to believe I was going to have to shoot him in the hind laig to catch him, when he made the mistake to trying to climb a tree. I rode up onto him before he could get out of rech, and reched up and got him by the laig and pulled him down, and his langwidge was painful to hear.

It was his own fault he slipped outa my hand, he kicked so vi'lent. I didn't go to drop him on his head.

But jest as I was reching down for him, I heard hosses running, and looked up and here come that derned Alderville posse busting through the bresh right on me. I'd lost so much time chasing Snake River they'd catched up with me. So I scooped him up and hung him over my saddle horn, because he was out cold, and headed for Apache River. Cap'n Kidd drawed away from them hosses like they was hobbled, so they warn't scarcely in pistol-range of us when we busted out on the east bank. The river was up, jest a-foaming and a-b'ling, and the footbridge warn't nothing only jest a log.

But Cap'n Kidd's sure-footed as a billy goat. We started acrost it, and everything went all right till we got about the middle of it, and then Snake River come to and seen the water booming along under us. He lost his head and begun to struggle and kick and holler, and his spurs scratched Cap'n Kidd's hide. That made Cap'n Kidd mad, and he turnt his head and tried to bite my laig, because he always blames me for everything that happens, and lost his balance and fell off.

That would of been all right, too, because as we hit the water I got hold of Cap'n Kidd's tail with one hand, and Snake River's undershirt with the other'n, and Cap'n Kidd hit out for the west bank. They is very few streams he cain't swim, flood or not. But jest as we was nearly acrost the posse appeared on the hind bank and started shooting at me, and they was apparently in some doubt as to which head in the water was me, because some of 'em shot at Snake River, too, jest to make sure. He opened his mouth to holler at 'em, and got it full of water and dern near strangled.

Then all to onst somebody in the bresh on the west shore opened up with a Winchester, and one of the posse hollered: "Look out, boys! It's a trap! Elkins has led us into a ambush!"

They turnt around and high-tailed it for Alderville.

WELL, WHAT WITH THE shooting and a gullet full of water, Snake River was having a regular fit and he kicked and thrashed so he kicked hisself clean out of his undershirt, and jest as my feet hit bottom, he slipped out of my grip and went whirling off downstream.

I jumped out on land, ignoring the hearty kick Cap'n Kidd planted in my midriff, and grabbed my lariat off my saddle. Gooseneck Wilkerson come prancing outa the bresh, waving a Winchester and yelling: "Don't let him drownd, dang you! My whole campaign depends on that spellin' bee! Do somethin'!"

I run along the bank and made a throw and looped Snake River around the ears. It warn't a very good catch, but the best I could do under the circumstances, and skin will always grow back onto a man's ears.

I hauled him out of the river, and it was plumb ungrateful for him to accuse me later of dragging him over them sharp rocks on purpose. I like to know how he figgered I could rope him outa Apache River without skinning him up a little. He'd swallered so much water he was nigh at his last gasp. Gooseneck rolled him onto his belly and jumped up and down on his back with both feet to git the water out; Gooseneck said that was artifishul respiration, but from the way Snake River hollered I don't believe it done him much good.

Anyway, he choked up several gallons of water. When he was able to threaten our lives betwixt cuss-words, Gooseneck says: "Git him on yore hoss and le's git started. Mine run off when the shootin' started. I jest suspected you'd be pursued by them dumb-wits and would take the short-cut. That's why I come to meet you. Come on. We got to git Snake River some medical attention. In his present state he ain't in no shape to conduck no spellin' match."

Snake River was too groggy to set in the saddle, so we hung him acrost it like a cow-hide over a fence, and started out, me leading Cap'n Kidd. It makes Cap'n Kidd very mad to have anybody but me on his back, so we hadn't went more'n a mile when he reched around and sot his teeth in the seat of Snake River's pants. Snake River had been groaning very weak and dismal and commanding us to stop and let him down so's he could utter his last words, but when Cap'n Kidd bit him he let out a remarkable strong yell and bust into langwidge unfit for a dying man.

"$%/#&!" quoth he passionately. "Why have I got to be butchered for a Yeller Dog holiday?"

We was reasoning with him, when Old Man Jake Hanson hove out of the bushes. Old Jake had a cabin a hundred yards back from the trail. He was about the width of a barn door, and his whiskers was marvelous to behold. "What's this ungodly noise about?" he demanded. "Who's gittin' murdered?"

"I am!" says Snake River fiercely. "I'm bein' sacrificed to the passions of the brutal mob!"

"You shet up," said Gooseneck severely. "Jake, this is the gent we've consented to let conduck the spellin' match."

"Well, well!" says Jake, interested. "A educated man, hey? Why, he don't look no different from us folks, if the blood war wiped offa him. Say, lissen, boys, bring him over to my cabin! I'll dress his wounds and feed him and take keer of him and git him to the city hall tomorrer night in time for the spellin' match. In the meantime he can teach my datter Salomey her letters."

"I refuse to tutor a dirty-faced cub--" began Snake River w hen he seen a face peeking eagerly at us from the trees. "Who's that?" he demanded.

"My datter Salomey," says Old Jake. "Nineteen her last birthday and cain't neither read nor write. None of my folks ever could, far back as family history goes, but I wants her to git some education."

"It's a human obligation," says Snake River. "I'll do it!"

So we left him at Jake's cabin, propped up on a bunk, with Salomey feeding him spoon-vittles and whiskey, and

me and Gooseneck headed for Yeller Dog, which warn't hardly a mile from there.

Gooseneck says to me: "We won't say nothin' about Snake River bein' at Jake's shack. Bull Hawkins is sweet on Salomey and he's so dern jealous-minded it makes him mad for another man to even stop there to say hello to the folks. We don't want nothin' to interfere with our show."

"You ack like you got a lot of confidence in it," I says.

"I banks on it heavy," says he. "It's a symbol of civilization."

WELL, JEST AS WE COME into town we met Mule McGrath with fire in his eye and corn-juice on his breath. "Gooseneck, lissen!" says he. "I jest got wind of a plot of Hawkins and Jack Clanton to git a lot of our voters so drunk election day that they won't be able to git to the polls. Le's call off the spellin' match and go over to the Red Tomahawk and clean out that rat-nest!"

"Naw," says Gooseneck, "we promised the mob a show, and we keeps our word. Don't worry; I'll think of a way to circumvent the heathen."

Mule headed back for the Silver Saddle, shaking his head, and Gooseneck sot down on the aidge of a hoss-trough and thunk deeply. I'd begun to think he'd drapped off to sleep, when he riz up and said: "Breck, git hold of Soapy Jackson and tell him to sneak out of camp and stay hid till the mornin' of the eleventh. Then he's to ride in jest before the polls open and spread the news that they has been a big gold strike over in Wild Ross Gulch. A lot of fellers will stampede for there without waitin' to vote. Meanwhile you will have circulated amongst the men you know air goin' to vote for me, and let 'em know we air goin' to work this campaign strategy. With all my men in camp, and most of Bull's headin' for Wild Ross Gulch, right and justice triumphs and I wins."

So I went and found Soapy and told him what Gooseneck said, and on the strength of it he imejitly headed for the Silver Saddle, and begun guzzling on campaign credit. I felt it was my duty to go along with him and see that he didn't get so full he forgot what he was supposed to do, and we was putting down the sixth dram apiece when in come Jack McDonald, Jim Leary, and Tarantula Allison, all Hawkins men. Soapy focused his wandering eyes on 'em, and says: "W-who's this here clutterin' up the scenery? Whyn't you mavericks stay over to the Red Tomahawk whar you belong?"

"It's a free country," asserted Jack McDonald. "What about this here derned spellin' match Gooseneck's braggin' about all over town?"

"Well, what about it?" I demanded, hitching my harness for'ard. The political foe don't live which can beard a Elkins in his lair.

16

"We demands to know who conducks it," stated Leary. "At least half the men in camp eligible to compete is in our crowd. We demands fair play!"

"We're bringin' in a cultured gent from another town," I says coldly.

"Who?" demanded Allison.

"None of yore dang business!" trumpeted Soapy, which gets delusions of valor when he's full of licker. "As a champion of progress and civic pride I challenges the skunk-odored forces of corrupt politics, and--"

Bam! McDonald swung with a billiard ball and Soapy kissed the sawdust.

"Now look what you done," I says peevishly. "If you coyotes cain't ack like gents, you'll oblige me by gittin' to hell outa here."

"If you don't like our company suppose you tries to put us out!" they challenged.

So when I'd finished my drink I taken their weppins away from 'em and throwed 'em headfirst out the side door. How was I to know somebody had jest put up a new cast-iron hitching-rack out there? Their friends carried 'em over to the Red Tomahawk to sew up their sculps, and I went back into the Silver Saddle to see if Soapy had come to yet. Jest as I reched the door he come weaving out, muttering in his whiskers and waving his six-shooter.

"Do you remember what all I told you?" I demanded.

17

"S-some of it!" he goggled, with his glassy eyes wobbling in all directions.

"Well, git goin' then," I urged, and helped him up onto his hoss. He left town at full speed, with both feet outa the stirrups and both arms around the hoss' neck.

"Drink is a curse and a delusion," I told the barkeep in disgust. "Look at that sickenin' example and take warnin'! Gimme me a bottle of rye."

WELL, GOOSENECK DONE a good job of advertising the show. By the middle of the next afternoon men was pouring into town from claims all up and down the creek. Half an hour before the match was sot to begin the hall was full. The benches was moved back from the front part, leaving a space clear all the way acrost the hall. They had been a lot of argyment about who was to compete, and who was to choose sides, but when it was finally settled, as satisfactory as anything ever was settled in Yeller Dog, they was twenty men to compete, and Lobo Harrison and Jack Clanton was to choose up.

By a peculiar coincidence, half of that twenty men was Gooseneck's, and half was Bull's. So naturally Lobo choosed his pals, and Clanton chosed his'n.

"I don't like this," Gooseneck whispered to me. "I'd ruther they'd been mixed up. This is beginnin' to look like a contest between my gang and Bull's. If they win, it'll make me look cheap. Where the hell is Snake River?"

18

"I ain't seen him," I said, "You ought to of made 'em take off their guns."

"Shucks," says he. "What could possibly stir up trouble at sech a lady-like affair as a spellin' bee. Dang it, where is Snake River? Old Jake said he'd git him here on time."

"Hey, Gooseneck!" yelled Bull Hawkins from where he sot amongst his coharts. "Why'n't you start the show?"

Bull was a big broad-shouldered hombre with black mustashes like a walrus. The crowd begun to holler and cuss and stomp their feet and this pleased Bull very much.

"Keep 'em amused," hissed Gooseneck. "I'll go look for Snake River."

He snuck out a side door and I riz up and addressed the throng. "Gents," I said, "be patient! They is a slight delay, but it won't be long. Meantime I'll be glad to entertain you all to the best of my ability. Would you like to hear me sing Barbary Allen?"

"No, by grab!" they answered in one beller.

"Well, yo're a-goin' to!" I roared, infuriated by this callous lack of the finer feelings. "I will now sing," I says, drawing my .45s "and I blows the brains out of the first coyote which tries to interrupt me."

I then sung my song without interference, and when I was through I bowed and waited for the applause, but all I heard was Lobo Harrison saying: "Imagine what the pore wolves on Bear Creek has to put up with!"

This cut me to the quick, but before I could make a suitable reply, Gooseneck slid in, breathing heavy. "I can't find Snake River," he hissed. "But the bar-keep gimme a book he found somewheres. Most of the leaves is tore out, but there's plenty left. I've marked some of the longest words, Breck. You can read good enough to give 'em out. You got to! If we don't start the show right away, this mob'll wreck the place. Yo're the only man not in the match which can even read a little, outside of me and Bull. It wouldn't look right for me to do it, and I shore ain't goin' to let Bull run my show."

I knew I was licked.

"Aw, well, all right," I said. "I might of knew I'd be the goat. Gimme the book."

"Here it is," he said. "'The Adventures of a French Countess.' Be dern shore you don't give out no words except them I marked."

"Hey!" bawled Jack Clanton. "We're gittin' tired standin' up here. Open the ball."

"All right," I says. "We commences."

"Hey!" said Bull. "Nobody told us Elkins was goin' to conduck the ceremony. We was told a cultured gent from outa town was to do it."

"Well," I says irritably, "Bear Creek is my home range, and I reckon I'm as cultured as any snake-hunter here. If anybody thinks he's better qualified than me, step up whilst I stomp his ears off."

Nobody volunteered, so I says "All right. I tosses a dollar to see who gits the first word." It fell for Harrison's gang, so I looked in the book at the first word marked, and it was a gal's name.

"Catharine," I says.

Nobody said nothing.

"Catharine!" I roared, glaring at Lobo Harrison.

"What you lookin' at me for?" he demanded. "I don't know no gal by that name."

"%$&*@!" I says with passion. "That's the word I give out. Spell it, dammit!"

"Oh," says he. "All right. K-a-t-h-a-r-i-n-n."

"That's wrong," I says.

"What you mean wrong?" he roared. "That's right!"

"'Tain't accordin' to the book," I said.

"Dang the book," says he. "I knows my rights and I ain't to be euchered by no ignorant grizzly from Bear Creek!"

"Who you callin' ignorant?" I demanded, stung, "Set down! You spelt it wrong."

"You lie!" he howled, and went for his gun. But I fired first.

WHEN THE SMOKE CLEARED away I seen everybody was on their feet preparing for to stampede, sech as warn't trying to crawl under the benches, so I said: "Set down, everybody. They ain't nothin' to git excited about. The spellin' match continues--and I'll shoot the first scoundrel which tries to leave the hall before the entertainment's over."

Gooseneck hissed fiercely at me: "Dammit, be careful who you shoot, cain't'cha? That was another one of my voters!"

"Drag him out!" I commanded, wiping off some blood where a slug had notched my ear. "The spellin' match is ready to commence again."

They was a kind of tension in the air, men shuffling their feet and twisting their mustashes and hitching their gun-belts, but I give no heed. I now approached the other side, with my hand on my pistol, and says to Clanton: "Can you spell Catharine?"

"C-a-t-h-a-r-i-n-e!" says he.

"Right, by golly!" I says, consulting The French Countess, and the audience cheered wildly and shot off their pistols into the roof.

"Hey!" says Bill Stark, on the other side. "That's wrong. Make him set down! It spells with a 'K'!"

"He spelt it jest like it is in the book," I says. "Look for yoreself."

"I don't give a damn!" he yelled, rudely knocking The French Countess outa my hand. "It's a misprint! It spells with a 'K' or they'll be more blood on the floor! He spelt it wrong and if he don't set down I shoots him down!"

"I'm runnin' this show!" I bellered, beginning to get mad. "You got to shoot me before you shoots anybody else!"

"With pleasure!" snarled he, and went for his gun.... Well, I hit him on the jaw with my fist and he went to sleep amongst a wreckage of busted benches. Gooseneck jumped up with a maddened shriek.

"Dang yore soul, Breckinridge!" he squalled. "Quit cancelin' my votes! Who air you workin' for--me or Hawkins?"

"Haw! haw! haw!" bellered Hawkins. "Go on with the show! This is the funniest thing I ever seen!"

Wham! The door crashed open and in pranced Old Jake Hanson, waving a shotgun.

"Welcome to the festivities, Jake," I greeted him, "Where's--"

"You son of a skunk!" quoth he, and let go at me with both barrels. The shot scattered remarkable. I didn't get more'n five or six of 'em and the rest distributed freely amongst the crowd. You ought to of heard 'em holler--the folks, I mean, not the buckshot.

"What in tarnation air you doin'?" shrieked Gooseneck. "Where's Snake River?"

"Gone!" howled Old Jake. "Run off! Eloped with my datter!"

Bull Hawkins riz with a howl of anguish, convulsively clutching his whiskers.

"Salomey?" he bellered. "Eloped?"

"With a cussed gambolier they brung over from Alderville!" bleated Old Jake, doing a war-dance in his passion. "Elkins and Wilkerson persuaded me to take that snake into my boozum! In spite of my pleas and protests they forced him into my peaceful $# %* household, and he stole the pore, mutton-headed innercent's blasted heart with his cultured airs and his slick talk! They've run off to git married!"

"It's a political plot!" shrieked Hawkins, going for his gun, "Wilkerson done it a-purpose!"

I shot the gun out of his hand, but Jack Clanton crashed a bench down on Gooseneck's head and Gooseneck kissed the floor. Clanton come down on top of him, out cold, as Mule McGrath swung with a pistol butt, and the next instant somebody lammed Mule with a brick bat and he flopped down acrost Clanton. And then the fight was on. Them rival political factions jest kind of riz up and rolled together in a wave of profanity, gun-smoke and splintering benches.

I HAVE ALWAYS NOTICED that the best thing to do in sech cases is to keep yore temper, and that's what I did for some time, in spite of the efforts of nine or ten wild-eyed Hawkinites. I didn't even shoot one of 'em; I kept my head and battered their skulls with a joist I tore outa the floor, and when I knocked 'em down I didn't stomp 'em hardly any. But they kept coming, and Jack McDonald was obsessed with the notion that he could ride me to the floor by jumping up astraddle of my neck. So he done it, and having discovered his idee was a hallucination, he got a fistful of my hair with his left, and started beating me in the head with his pistol-barrel.

It was very annoying. Simultaneous, several other misfits got hold of my laigs, trying to rassle me down, and some son of Baliol stomped severely on my toe. I had bore my afflictions as patient as Job up to that time, but this perfidy maddened me.

I give a roar which loosened the shingles on the roof, and kicked the toe-stomper in the belly with sech fury that he curled up on the floor with a holler groan and taken no more interest in the proceedings. I likewise busted my timber on somebody's skull, and reched up and pulled Jack McDonald off my neck like pulling a tick off a bull's hide, and hev him through a convenient winder. He's a liar when he says I aimed him deliberate at that rain barrel. I didn't even know they was a rain barrel till I heard his head crash through the staves. I then shaken nine or ten idjits loose from my shoulders and shook the blood outa my eyes and

25

preceived that Gooseneck's men was getting the worst of it, particularly including Gooseneck hisself. So I give another roar and prepared to wade through them fool Hawkinites like a b'ar through a pack of hound-dogs, when I discovered that some perfidious side-winder had got my spur tangled in his whiskers.

I stooped to ontangle myself, jest as a charge of buckshot ripped through the air where my head had been a instant before. Three or four critters was rushing me with bowie knives, so I give a wrench and tore loose by main force. How could I help it if most of the whiskers come loose too? I grabbed me a bench to use for a club, and I mowed the whole first rank down with one swipe, and then as I drawed back for another lick, I heard somebody yelling above the melee.

"Gold!" he shrieked.

Everybody stopped like they was froze in their tracks. Even Bull Hawkins shook the blood outa his eyes and glared up from where he was kneeling on Gooseneck's wishbone with one hand in Gooseneck's hair and a bowie in the other'n. Everybody quit fighting everybody else, and looked at the door--and there was Soapy Jackson, a-reeling and a-weaving with a empty bottle in one hand, and hollering.

"Big gold strike in Wild Hoss Gulch," he blats. "Biggest the West ever seen! Nuggets the size of osteridge aigs--gulp!"

He disappeared in a wave of frenzied humanity as Yeller
Dog's population abandoned the fray and headed for the
wide open spaces. Even Hawkins ceased his efforts to sculp
Gooseneck alive and j'ined the stampede. They tore the
whole front out of the city hall in their flight, and even them
which had been knocked stiff come to at the howl of "Gold!"
and staggered wildly after the mob, shrieking pitifully for
their picks, shovels and jackasses. When the dust had settled
and the thunder of boot-heels had faded in the distance, the
only human left in the city hall was me and Gooseneck, and
Soapy Jackson, which riz unsteadily with the prints of hob-
nails all over his homely face. They shore trompled him free
and generous in their rush.

Gooseneck staggered up, glared wildly about him, and
went into convulsions. At first he couldn't talk at all; he jest
frothed at the mouth. When he found speech his langwidge
was shocking.

"What you spring it this time of night for?" he howled.
"Breckinridge, I said tell him to bring the news in the
mornin', not tonight!"

"I did tell him that," I says.

"Oh, so that was what I couldn't remember!" says Soapy.
"That lick McDonald gimme so plumb addled my brains I
knowed they was somethin' I forgot, but couldn't remember
what it was."

"Oh sole mio!" gibbered Gooseneck, or words to that effeck.

"Well, what you kickin' about?" I demanded peevishly, having jest discovered that somebody had stabbed me in the hind laig during the melee. My boot was full of blood, and they was brand-new boots. "It worked, didn't it?" I says. "They're all headin' for Wild Hoss Gulch, includin' Hawkins hisself, and they cain't possibly git back afore day after tomorrer."

"Yeah!" raved Gooseneck. "They're all gone, includin' my gang! The damn camp's empty! How can I git elected with nobody here to hold the election, and nobody to vote?"

"Oh," I says. "That's right. I hadn't thunk of that."

He fixed me with a awful eye.

"Did you," says he in a blood-curdling voice, "did you tell my voters Soapy was goin' to enact a political strategy?"

"By golly!" I said. "You know it plumb slipped my mind! Ain't that a joke on me?"

"Git out of my life!" says Gooseneck, drawing his gun.

That was a genteel way for him to ack, trying to shoot me after all I'd did for him! I taken his gun away from him as gentle as I knowed how and it was his own fault he got his arm broke. But to hear him rave you would of thought he considered I was to blame for his misfortunes or something. I was so derned disgusted I clumb onto Cap'n Kidd and shaken the dust of that there camp offa my boots, because I seen they was no gratitude in Yeller Dog.

I likewise seen I wasn't cut out for the skullduggery of politics. I had me a notion one time that I'd make a hiyu sheriff but I learnt my lesson. It's like my pap says, I reckon.

"All the law a man needs," says he, "is a gun tucked into his pants. And the main l'arnin' he needs is to know which end of that gun the bullet comes out of."

What's good enough for pap, gents, is good enough for me.

www.ingramcontent.com/pod-product-compliance
Lightning Source LLC
Chambersburg PA
CBHW030243180626
46810CB00008B/3265